SACRAMENTO PUBLIC LIBRARY

D0402055

JoJo

(QUEEN DJ AND BOWBOW)

BY JOJO SIWA

AMULET BOOKS
NEW YORK

PUBLISHER'S NOTE: This is a work of fiction. Names, characters, places, and incidents are either the product of the author's imagination or used fictitiously, and any resemblance to actual persons, living or dead, business establishments, events, or locales is entirely coincidental.

Cataloging-in-Publication Data has been applied for and may be obtained from the Library of Congress.

ISBN 978-1-4197-4598-0

Text copyright © 2020 JoJo Siwa
Cover and illustrations copyright © 2020 Abrams Books
Book design by Siobhan Gallagher
© 2020 Viacom International Inc. All rights reserved. Nickelodeon and all related titles and logos are trademarks of Viacom International Inc. JoJo Siwa is a trademark of JoJo Siwa Entertainment, LLC.

Published in 2020 by Amulet Books, an imprint of ABRAMS. All rights reserved. No portion of this book may be reproduced, stored in a retrieval system, or transmitted in any form or by any means, mechanical, electronic, photocopying, recording, or otherwise, without written permission from the publisher.

Printed and bound in the United States
10 9 8 7 6 5 4 3 2 1

Amulet Books are available at special discounts when purchased in quantity for premiums and promotions as well as fundraising or educational use. Special editions can also be created to specification. For details, contact specialsales@abramsbooks.com or the address below.

Amulet Books® is a registered trademark of Harry N. Abrams, Inc.

ABRAMS The Art of Books
195 Broadway, New York, NY 10007
abramsbooks.com

CONTENTS

CHAPTER 1

"JoJo, we're nearly there!" JoJo blinked and rubbed sleep from her eyes, then turned to meet her best friend's excited smile with one of her own. Miley was practically jumping up and down, or at least as much as she could underneath her seat belt in the back of her mom's car. "I can't believe this is my first time ever at sleepaway camp!" Miley exclaimed.

"Except when you were a baby," her mom corrected from the front seat.

"Mom! That doesn't count." Miley's mom had filled them in on the story when they'd set off earlier that day: When Miley was just a baby, her mom and dad had taken her to Joshua Tree, a national park in California, to go camping. Miley had tried to snuggle up with a spider that snuck into their cabin! The spider hadn't been poisonous, but her mom had snatched Miley up and run outside in her pajamas while Miley's dad fended off the perfectly harmless spider.

"Poor spider," Miley added.

"Oh, it eventually crawled off. Your father just frightened it—he wouldn't hurt a fly," Miley's mom assured the girls.

"The spider would hurt a fly," Miley joked.

"I would have run too," JoJo told Miley's mom. "Miley, you've always been fearless!"

"Let's hope this weekend is light on spiders and heavy on s'mores," Miley joked. "I'm so glad you came with me, JoJo."

"You girls are going to have a great time," said Miley's mom. "Miley, I'm so proud of you for joining the Art Stars. Did you know some of the best choreographers in the world came out of this program?"

"And dancers, and musicians . . . the list goes on!" JoJo exclaimed. She was proud of her best friend too. The Art Stars was a performing arts organization for girls that Miley had been selected to join because she was such an amazingly talented choreographer. JoJo would know—Miley had choreographed some of JoJo's own routines! The organization hosted lots of weekend events and activities for its members throughout the year, and the kickoff event took place over one weekend every spring at a national park in Northern

California. Miley had asked if JoJo could attend as her special guest, and the camp director had agreed since JoJo was a talented performer in her own right.

The car took a left on to a long gravel driveway lined with pine trees.

"This is so exciting," JoJo said, craning her neck to try to see the tops of the trees. "Can you believe there's even going to be horse-back riding?"

"Now I miss Dusty!" Miley exclaimed.

"Dusty will be just fine for the weekend," Miley's mom told her. "Your dad and I will go visit her at the ranch while you're gone. And she'll be waiting for you when you come home."

"Thanks, Mom." Miley beamed. Dusty, her miniature pony, had been a birthday gift, and Miley was madly in love with her. JoJo had to admit—Dusty was pretty cute. The pony was no BowBow, of course—but then, no one was cuter than her fluffy little Yorkie. JoJo totally got it though. Pets were the best! She was going to miss BowBow like crazy all weekend!

The car reached the end of the drive and pulled up in front of a long log cabin. A banner hanging across the front of the cabin read WELCOME, ART STARS!

Miley squealed and clapped her hands. "I wonder who our counselors will be!"

Before JoJo could answer, a woman with curly brown hair approached the car, and Miley's mom rolled down her window.

"Are you here for the Art Stars' opening weekend?" the woman asked with a friendly smile.

Before her mom could answer, Miley yelled, "*We* are!" and pointed to herself and JoJo. JoJo smiled and waved from beside her. She loved seeing her BFF so happy.

The woman laughed and said, "Well then you're in the right spot! You can park just over there"—she motioned to a gravel-covered patch to the left of the building—"and come straight into the office, just there inside the cabin, when you're ready. I'll let you know your bunk assignments and what to expect from the rest of today. I'm Bethany, by the way—I'm the director of the Art Stars program."

"So nice to meet you." Miley's mom gave Bethany a big smile. "We'll be right in!"

Miley's mom left the window down, and JoJo breathed in the fresh air as they pulled into the parking spot. It was so different from their neighborhood back home, which was smack in the middle of a big city—it even smelled different! She could feel her skin tingle in anticipation of all the fun they were about to have. It was a whole new adventure! And best of all, it signaled they were getting older. JoJo had given performances on tour all over the country, but always with her mom at her side. Sleepaway camp—no moms allowed—was a first for her too.

Once they got out of the car, the girls shrugged on their backpacks—JoJo's was covered in glitter and bows, Miley's in pink and purple sequins—and headed for the cabin, with Miley's mom in tow. "I'll leave just as soon as I help you girls get settled in your cabin," she told them.

Bethany was waiting with two folders—one with each of their names—when JoJo and Miley walked into the building. The walls of the main office were covered in posters of famous ice skaters and dancers and Broadway choreographers.

"Those are all camp alums," Bethany told the girls, following their gazes.

"Really?" Miley's voice was low with awe.

"Yep! Everyone on these walls was once an Art Star."

"That is so cool," JoJo told Miley. Miley nodded, beaming.

Bethany gestured for JoJo, Miley, and Miley's mom to take a seat. After she handed them their welcome packets, she took a seat too. "The best part of this camp is that we bring back former campers as counselors to help guide and mentor new campers. Most of them are in high school now. I won't tell you who's here this year, but we have a great group! They'll be joining you at the opening-night pizza party in an hour in the party barn. For now, let me go over the program rules and then we'll find your cabin assignments."

Mmm, pizza party, thought JoJo, as Bethany began going over all the rules. There were a lot of them, like: "No going out unsupervised after dark," "Stick with a counselor on hikes," "Buddy system always," and stuff like that. JoJo listened carefully—she wanted to be sure not to miss anything important.

"Are there any spiders?" JoJo wanted to know. She winked at Miley.

Bethany laughed. "I'm sure there are, but if you're lucky you won't see one! Most critters stay away from campers—they're as afraid of us as we are of them. But don't worry, you'll learn Survival Skills 101 while you're here, just in case. Now follow me! Let's get you settled in your cabin."

JoJo and Miley lugged their overstuffed backpacks while Miley's mom trailed behind with their sleeping bags. JoJo had brought her favorite sleeping bag. It was pink and covered in bows, cupcakes, ice cream, and doughnuts. Miley had a sleeping bag with a rainbow and unicorn, borrowed from their friend Grace. (Unicorns—and lately caticorns—were Grace's favorite thing!)

"You're the first ones here," Bethany told them once they reached the cabin. "You'll have two other campers in here." She gestured to the three sets of bunk beds arranged against three of the cabin walls. "You get first choice of bunks, lucky you! And you each have a personal locker over there"—she pointed to the wall across from them—"where you can store your belongings. Your keys are in the locks."

JoJo went over to one of the lockers and noticed that the keys were attached to stretchy wristbands, woven with pink and gold glitter, almost like cute friendship bracelets. "Love it!" she exclaimed.

"Those are waterproof and can stay on

your wrists at all times," Bethany said. "But if you have anything valuable that you want kept in the main office, that's fine too. We ask campers to leave your phones in the lockbox in the main office. Phones get easily lost at camp, and the signal is iffy anyway since we don't have Wi-Fi outside the main office. You can access them to call your parents anytime you like."

JoJo thought about it. She had her cell phone, but all she'd use it for would be photos. She decided it made sense to keep it in the office. She pulled it from her back pocket and handed it to Bethany, and Miley did the same.

"It's just you and me, girl," Miley told her, wrapping her arms around JoJo's shoulder. "It's about to get real."

"Will someone be taking photos?" JoJo

asked Bethany. "I have a feeling this will be a weekend I'll want to remember!"

"I will," Bethany assured her. "And there will be a slideshow at the end of the weekend."

"Great!" Miley exclaimed.

"On that note, I'm going to let you two get settled," Miley's mom told them, smiling. "I can see you're in good hands. Thanks, Bethany," she said, turning to the other woman. "Miley, I'll be back on Sunday afternoon to pick up you and JoJo and see the talent show. If either of you need to reach me, you can call me from your cell phone in the main office."

"Hold up—talent show?" Miley wanted to know.

"Yes," her mom said. "I wanted that part to be a surprise! I knew if I told you," she said with a laugh, "you'd have planned your routine months ago."

"Truth," Miley said, giggling. "I would have obsessed over it. Thanks for the ride, Mom!" She gave her mom a huge hug, then peeked out at JoJo and waved her over. "Come on, JoJo!"

JoJo ran over to join them and wrapped her arms tightly around Miley and Miley's mom, who was like her second mom. For a brief moment, she felt a flash of home-sickness. What would they do without their moms, Dusty, and BowBow for two whole days?

The girls broke away from Miley's mom, who left the cabin and headed back toward the car, then turned and blew them a kiss. Miley grabbed JoJo's hand—it was as if she could read her mind.

"Don't worry," Miley told JoJo. "We've got each other."

But JoJo's gaze had fallen on another girl,

a few years older, who was walking toward them.

"We've got each other . . . and we've got *Belle*, it looks like," she whispered to Miley.

Miley frowned in confusion. "What are you—"

A high-pitched voice, extra-bright, cut Miley off.

"Oh *hi*, JoJo!" the voice squealed. "Look at you! You don't look any different at all! Still the same hairdo. That's cute." The girl was wearing a hot pink one-piece bathing suit with denim cutoffs, multicolored sneakers, and giant heart-shaped sunglasses. Her light brown hair was pulled back in a bun atop her head.

"Oh! You girls know each other already—fantastic!" Bethany clapped, delighted, and turned to the younger girls. "Miley and JoJo, Belle Manning is one of the mentor counselors. She'll be the bunk leader of the cabin right next to yours. I'll let you girls get reacquainted—see you at pizza! There are signs to the party barn along the path just outside your cabin." Bethany walked off, leaving the girls alone.

"Hi, Belle," JoJo said in a friendly tone, as Miley's eyes widened in understanding. JoJo had told Miley all about Belle, who had been the meanest girl at a competitive dance workshop JoJo had taken the year before.

Belle stepped inside and leaned over to hug JoJo. "Queen B in the house!" she squealed. Then her gaze roamed around their cabin. "Looks like you've got top bunk, JoJo, judging by that sleeping bag. You *would* have something covered in bows. Love it," she said, sounding like she didn't love it. "And that means *you* must have bottom bunk." She motioned to Miley, who nodded. "Great. Good to know. I like to keep an eye on things," she explained, as JoJo fought to keep her expression neutral.

"Now excuse me while I put my stuff down next door." She brushed past JoJo and headed outside. The girls followed her out, watching as she entered her own cabin. JoJo saw Belle pick up a backpack from a bed—probably left by another camper—and toss it onto the floor. Then she put her things on top of the bunk where the backpack had been. With three sets of bunks there were plenty of beds to go around, but Belle apparently wanted *that* specific one.

"This is just perfect," she called to the girls, as she spread out her sleeping bag. "What a great weekend, amiright?" She laughed and clapped her hands—but if you asked JoJo, there was nothing funny about that other camper's backpack lying on its side on the

16

floor of Belle's cabin. JoJo and Miley exchanged a look. It was a look only the two of them could understand, but it was one they used often. It meant, *What have we gotten ourselves into this time?*

CHAPTER 2

"**A**t least she's not in *our* cabin," Miley pointed out, as she and JoJo made their way toward the party barn for the welcome pizza party. "It could be a lot worse."

"True," JoJo said. "And who knows. Dance workshop was a long time ago—maybe Belle has changed." Miley looked doubtful, but there was no time to talk about it more because a friendly girl with blond hair wearing an orange Art Stars T-shirt was waving at them from the entrance of the party barn.

"Welcome!" she said. "I'm Margot. We're about to get started! Wait a sec . . . Aren't you . . . ?" She peered closely at JoJo. "No way! JoJo Siwa! I'm a huge fan," she gushed. "I'm so excited you're here!" She pointed to her full, blond hair, which was pulled up into a side ponytail. "Left my bow at home, but I'm rocking the side pony, as always. I love your style."

"Thanks!" JoJo said. "And don't worry, I have plenty of extra bows back in the cabin, if you want one. This is my friend Miley. She's one of the most talented choreographers I know. I'm just along for the ride this weekend." JoJo always tried to build up her friends when people recognized her—she didn't like stealing the show. And this was Miley's weekend, not hers.

"Awesome," said Margot. She smiled

warmly at Miley, and her cheeks dimpled. "Maybe we'll get to see your choreography at the talent show Sunday."

"For sure," Miley told her. "I can't wait! But where's the pizza?"

JoJo laughed. When Miley was hungry, nothing could stop her. Margot waved them through the entrance of the barn. Hay bales served as seats at long wooden tables that were covered in piping-hot pizzas. Friendly looking teenagers wearing orange T-shirts helped their campers load up plates and pour soda into paper cups. JoJo eyed the pizza selection. There was pepperoni, cheese, veggie . . . everything they could want. Miley and JoJo grabbed paper plates and made a beeline for the cheese pizza. JoJo was reaching for a slice when she heard, "JoJo?" in a friendly tone.

She put on a smile and prepared to greet a fan—but was totally surprised when she lifted her gaze to meet that of a very familiar face. "Jamilla, no way!" JoJo dropped her pizza on a plate and gave her friend a huge hug. Jamilla had been in the same dance workshop where JoJo had met Belle. Jamilla was a professional ballerina and one of the nicest girls JoJo had ever met. She was a few years older than JoJo and had stayed away from the drama Belle had caused back in the workshop. JoJo and Jamilla had remained close through Snapchat and FaceTime and Instagram, but JoJo hadn't seen her friend in ages.

"Hi, Miley!" Jamilla exclaimed. She'd met Miley too, and the two of them had completely clicked. "It's so great to see you both here!"

"What a cool surprise," Miley said, reaching over to hug Jamilla, whose warm smile lit up her face again. "Great to see you, girl."

"I'm actually not surprised," Jamilla said

with a sneaky smile. "I'm a mentor coun-selor. I knew you'd both be here! I got my bunk assignments and saw your names on the list!"

"No way!" JoJo squealed and jumped up and down. "You're our counselor?! I was already so excited about this weekend, but I am a million times more excited now!"

"Yep!" The teenager helped herself to a slice of cheese pizza and a slice of mushroom. She motioned to JoJo and Miley to follow her to an open table, and the three settled onto hay bales.

"This straw is itchy," Miley announced. "I am so not comfortable."

Jamilla laughed. "It's better with jeans on," she said. "Pro tip."

"So wait, you were an Art Star when you were our age?" JoJo wanted to know. "Tell me everything." She took a giant bite of pizza and tilted her head back, savoring the cheesy goodness. Around them, more campers were starting to file into the room, which buzzed with laughter and excitement.

"I sure was," Jamilla said. "Belle, Bahi, and I were all Art Stars—we didn't ever cross paths here when we were campers, though. I guess Bethany, the woman who runs the Art Stars, is friends with Roberta Robbins—you remember her?"

"Of course." JoJo nodded, then explained to Miley, "She's a Broadway dance legend and was the leader of our dance workshop where we all met."

"Yeah, so, we did another workshop later that year—I think you were on tour, JoJo," Jamilla guessed. "And Bethany came by one day to say hi—I guess she was the one who recommended us all for the workshop in the first place!"

"That's so cool," Miley commented. "I'd love to be a counselor one day."

"You'd be a great one!" JoJo said. It was true. Miley was one of the best leaders she knew.

"I've really been looking forward to it myself," Jamilla confided. "But I got way more excited when I saw you two would be here."

"Are Bahi and Belle still close?" JoJo asked carefully.

"I think so," Jamilla said, polishing off her pizza and wiping her mouth. "Pretty sure they're still doing that Queen B thing." Jamilla was referring to Belle's nickname for herself and her friends—the one she'd used when she arrived. "But don't worry. Art Stars is a way bigger group than dance workshop was. She won't have a chance to pull any of her old tricks."

"She sort of already has," Miley piped

in. Jamilla scrunched her forehead and looked like she was about to ask what Miley meant, but just then, Belle strutted over with Bahi in tow. Both were carrying plates piled high with pizza slices. Bahi was just as beautiful as ever with her warm brown skin and shiny black hair draped over one shoulder.

"JoJo! Jamilla! Hi!" Bahi exclaimed. "When Belle said she had a surprise, I had no idea it would be you guys. Can we sit?"

"Sure," JoJo said, scooting over to make room. JoJo really liked Bahi. She was a super talented dancer who picked up routines faster than anyone. And she was genuinely nice. JoJo wasn't totally sure what tied Bahi and Belle together, other than that they'd been friends for a long time.

"And you're Miley, right?" Bahi asked, leaning over the table to offer Miley a grin. "I remember you from the Valentine's Day party at Michelle Lee's house!" She was referring to the amazing party that had capped off their dance workshop.

Miley nodded. "That's me. Great to see you again, Bahi."

"Is Michelle coming to camp?" JoJo wanted to know. She'd really liked the professional ice dancer—Michelle had been the nicest girl at workshop.

"No," Bahi said sadly. "I wish!" Then she brightened. "She's busy training for the next Olympics."

"So cool," breathed Miley. JoJo nodded in agreement.

"Miley," Bahi continued, "JoJo told us all at the workshop how amazing your choreography is. I'd love to check out your work."

"Sounds like we might have a chance at the talent show," Jamilla piped in.

"I heard the talent show is a contest," Belle contributed.

"I don't think so," Miley said, looking doubtful. "In fact, I thought the whole point of this camp was to get us all together while taking away the competitive element we always face in our performing lives."

JoJo nodded. That had been one of the big reasons they'd wanted to come—a chance to get away from contests and just relax and have fun with other girls from the dance community.

"Well it *should* be a contest," Belle said. "I already checked out my girls' résumés. We have it in the bag."

JoJo tried hard not to sigh. Belle always had to be the best—it was her thing. Even though the talent show wasn't a real contest, she seemed determined to make it one.

"I already gave all my campers 'B'

nicknames," Belle continued. "So we can all be the Queen Bs. Isn't that cute?" She looked at Bahi, clearly expecting her to agree. Bahi suddenly became very interested in her pizza, and her cheeks had reddened a little. JoJo caught her eye and gave her a little smile. It was then that she noticed Jamilla and Bahi were wearing orange Art Stars T-shirts like Margot had on, but Belle was still in her pink one-piece and shorts.

"Belle, why aren't you wearing the counselor shirt?" JoJo asked curiously.

"Gross," Belle said, her mouth full of pizza. "No one looks good in orange." She gave Jamilla a pointed look.

"I don't know, I'm feeling pretty fly," Jamilla said mildly. "Are you going swimming later, Belle?"

Belle narrowed her eyes and opened her mouth to retort.

"Well I think we'd better get back to our bunk," JoJo said, before Belle could answer. "Miley and I still haven't met our bunkmates."

"I'll come with you," Jamilla told them. "I'd love to meet the other girls now."

"Whew," Miley said as soon as they exited the barn and headed back along the narrow dirt path to the cabins. "That Belle is fierce."

"I don't love how she's trying to make the talent show into a competition," JoJo said, a tiny bit of dread making the pizza hop around in her stomach. "I like the idea of everyone being on equal footing and just having fun."

"Yeah. There's no need to turn it into a contest," Jamilla said. "There is no winner. In the past all the parents who come to watch have donated a little bit for a ticket to the show," she explained. "And the ticket profits go to a charity for dancers with disabilities. Helping other people is the real prize."

"We should still do our best," Miley pointed out. "Especially since the parents will expect a good show."

"Totally," Jamilla agreed. "We'll give it all we've got. But in the end, we're just here to have fun. Starting with s'mores around the campfire tonight!"

"Remember that one time," Miley started, "when I tried to make a s'more and—"

"You got marshmallow in your hair and your mom had to cut your hair short—" JoJo continued.

"Except just a chunk in the back, so I had a mini mullet for a week?" Miley snort-laughed.

"Oh yeah, I remember." JoJo giggled.

"I'll be steering clear of your marshmallow stick," Jamilla said, laughing, as they entered the cabin.

Two slightly younger girls with identical broad smiles and delicate features turned toward them. One was braiding her waist-length black hair, and the other was putting socks and underwear in the tall dresser that stood against the far wall.

"Hi!" they said in unison. Then stopped. Then, "Hi," they said again. "Jinx."

"Oh em gee, you first," the girl with the socks told the other one. "Sorry." She rolled her eyes. "We always do that. It can get annoying."

"I'm Sydney." The girl with the braid gestured at herself. "And this is Reagan, my twin sister. And *you're* JoJo Siwa!" Sydney exclaimed. "I knew camp was going to be cool, but this is So. Freaking. Cool. Rae-Rae, I can't believe we're sharing a cabin with JoJo Siwa."

"You're a bigger JoJo fan than I am," Reagan said generously. "I can't believe it, but you probably can't believe it even more."

Sydney nodded in agreement. "That's true," she said.

Jamilla cleared her throat. JoJo was glad. She loved making new friends, but sometimes people acted like they already knew her, even when they'd just met her. And this was Miley's weekend—JoJo was supposed to just be along for the ride.

"I'm Jamilla, your counselor," Jamilla told them. "And this is Miley." Miley waved.

"Nice to meet you guys," Miley said. "It's so cool that you're twins. When JoJo and I were younger, we used to pretend to be twins."

JoJo laughed. "True story. We dressed alike all the time and told people to call us by each other's names . . . even though we look nothing alike."

"Hi, Miley!" the twins said. Then Reagan asked, "Are you a dancer too?"

"Nope. Choreographer," Miley explained.

"So cool," Sydney said. "I've never met a choreographer our age. We do ballroom dance."

"That's awesome," Jamilla said. "Ballroom is such a cool specialty."

"We also do hip-hop and Bollywood," Reagan added. JoJo smiled at her. She could tell she was going to like these two—they were so full of energy!

"Let's talk more around the campfire," Jamilla suggested. "It's starting to get dark."

Sure enough, it was already sunset. JoJo couldn't believe how quickly their first day had gone! They only had Saturday and Sunday after this. She felt like camp was passing by too fast!

The girls grabbed sweatshirts—the twins

had on identical sequined zebra shirts and JoJo wondered how she'd ever tell them apart—and followed Jamilla along the path in the opposite direction from the party barn. Jamilla was carrying a flashlight, and she flicked it on when the trees became thicker alongside the path. Soon the trees were so thick, all JoJo could make out was the beam of the flashlight.

"Oooooo," a voice said in her ear.

JoJo jumped and squealed. "NOT funny, Miley," she said, while Miley dissolved in laughter. JoJo shivered. It was so dark amid the trees. When would they get to . . . ?

Then the trees broke, and JoJo saw the most beautiful sight ever.

There was a huge lake in front of them. There were stars everywhere. And over the water, there were hundreds of fire-flies lighting up the sky. It was hard to tell where the fireflies started and the stars ended!

"Whoa," the twins said, with a collective gasp.

"JoJo, have you ever seen anything like this in your life?" Miley wanted to know.

"Nope," JoJo said, taking it all in. "And look—there's the campfire!" She'd been so caught up at the sight of the lake and its dazzling guests of honor that she almost missed the campfire a few yards away. Lots of kids were already gathered around it with their counselors—probably a few dozen—roasting marshmallows and talking.

"Everyone, find yourself a stick," Jamilla instructed. She bent over some fallen branches at the edge of the trees and selected one for herself, and JoJo followed suit. Soon all four girls plus Jamilla had sticks—Sydney and Reagan had one to share.

"We share everything," Sydney explained.

Jamilla laughed. "Whatever works for you!" she said. "Now come on! Let's meet the other counselors and cadets!"

"This is Benji, Beth, Brit, and Bitsy," JoJo heard Belle telling someone as she approached.

"My name isn't Beth," one camper said to another, sounding confused. "It's Elizabeth. I go by Liz."

"Just go with it," the other camper whispered back. "My name is Mitzi, not Bitsy. And Benji's real name is Madeleine!"

JoJo sighed. Belle was definitely doing things *her* way. She hoped the campers could stand up to Belle! She remembered how Belle had insisted on calling Gabrielle from workshop "Bree" until Gabrielle gathered the courage to stand up to her. JoJo and Miley headed to the opposite side of the fire, where s'mores ingredients were spread out on a table. They each placed two marshmallows on their sticks. Next to them, Sydney and Reagan were trying to roast four at once. One melted off and fell into the fire.

"Oops," Reagan said. "Man down!" They both giggled.

When everyone had made and eaten at least one s'more, Bethany stood in front of the group, illuminating her face with a flashlight.

"Creepy!" a camper shouted, and the others giggled. JoJo shivered—it *was* a little spooky hanging out at night! But it was also exciting and cozy to be surrounded by talented girls who loved performing . . .

. . . Maybe a little *too* much. Just then, JoJo saw Belle sneaking up behind Bethany.

"Welcome, campers, to your very first Art Stars weekend!" Bethany was saying. Belle stood behind her and mimicked Bethany's facial expressions and movements, exaggerating them to look silly. Some of the campers laughed uncertainly, but JoJo noticed a counselor with short, curly hair frowning at Belle.

Then Belle shouted "Boo!" at the top of her lungs. Bethany jumped and gasped—then, seeing Belle, smiled tolerantly. "Back to your log, Belle," she said. "My welcome speech is for counselors too."

JoJo exchanged a glance with Miley when Belle froze, looking as if she was going to argue. Then Bahi motioned to Belle and patted the spot next to her on the log, offering a big smile. JoJo breathed a sigh of relief when Belle sat next to her friend.

"I hope you all have an amazing time this weekend," Bethany continued. "You're all hugely talented performers, and we are looking forward to seeing you showcase your talents on Sunday. But for now, this weekend is about bonding with like-minded creatives in a setting that's different from what you're used to. A lot of you are used to competing—but at Art Stars, the way to win is to just have fun!"

The girls cheered. JoJo glanced over at Belle, who was the only one not smiling and clapping. JoJo wondered why—so many of them were always performing on a stage or competing in front of an audience. It was really nice to have a break and get to know other artists on different terms. What could Belle be scowling about? Then she remembered. Belle liked to *win*. She liked to be the very best. So in a situation where everyone was on equal footing, she probably felt uncomfortable.

Well, JoJo thought to herself, *maybe it'll be good for Belle to mix things up.*

Bethany went on to explain that there

would be a "buddy bunk" system, so all thirty-six campers wouldn't be doing the same activities at once. Instead, they would rotate activities in groups of twelve. After Bethany's opening speech, the group sang a few songs and marched back to their cabins to wash up and put on their pajamas.

"We have to be up early tomorrow," Jamilla explained to Miley, JoJo, and the twins. "Breakfast is at 8 A.M."

"Nooo," JoJo groaned. She loved to sleep in.

"But there will be chocolate-chip pancakes," Jamilla added. "And tug-of-war after that! And guess what? I requested to be buddy bunks with Bahi's and Belle's groups. So we'll be doing all our activities with them."

"I'm okay with that!" JoJo laughed. She pulled on her favorite heart-covered pajama pants and matching tee and snuggled into her warm sleeping bag. Across from her, the

40

twins were settling in, and above her, Miley peeked over the edge of her top bunk. Jamilla was turning out the lights and readying her own bunk—the bottom of an empty one—on the room's opposite end.

"Love you, friend," Miley whispered to JoJo. JoJo blew her a kiss just before the lights went out. Within a minute, everyone in the bunk was snoring . . . except JoJo. She was so excited to ride horses and play volleyball and make crafts and kayak the next day. So what was it that was worrying her?

JoJo looked through the cabin window at the light still streaming from the cabin next door. Belle's shadow moved across the window as she reached to turn out the light, just as Jamilla had done. As she began to nod off, JoJo realized the source of her discomfort: She knew Belle was competitive. But just how far would her frenemy go to be top dog?

CHAPTER 3

The next morning, the girls were still full from giant stacks of chocolate-chip pancakes drenched in extra syrup, but definitely *not* too full to play tug-of-war and then meet the horses at the stables.

"I ate ten million pancakes," Miley said as they spotted the long rope, which was laid out in the field behind their cabins. Bethany stood a few feet away and waved at the girls as they approached. "My pancakes alone could win this contest."

"Think again," Belle trilled, skipping over to the rope. She pointed at her chest. "I'm appointing myself team captain," she said. "And I've got this end of the rope."

"Why do you care which end of the rope you have?" Bahi wanted to know.

A strange look crossed Belle's features, then she shrugged. "I just like this side," she told them. "It's my spirit side. Here, Bahi, you're on my team. Stand behind me."

"Okay then," Bethany said, laughing. "I guess I'll appoint Jamilla captain number two."

"Great!" Jamilla said as she faced the rest of the group. "Miley, you're on my team." Miley agreeably walked over to the older girl, and Belle and Jamilla continued to choose teams until all the girls were chosen. JoJo wound up on Miley and Jamilla's team. There was a big line of girls on one side of the rope, and a big line on the other side—about forty girls in all. JoJo thought they looked pretty evenly matched in terms of height and size. The rope lay at their feet. Belle rubbed her palms together, eager to begin.

"When I blow my whistle, you can all pick up the rope and begin tugging," Bethany told them. "And the prize for the winner is . . . no after-dinner cleanup!" She lifted her whistle to her mouth, and the girls crouched down, ready to grab the rope. "One . . . two . . . three!" She blew into the whistle, and the girls went wild.

JoJo reached down for the rope and felt her hands encounter something slick. "Hey!" she said, pulling away, just as behind her, Miley muttered, "What the . . . ?" JoJo looked back and noticed that all the girls on her side were struggling to keep hold of the rope. Maybe this was a twist Bethany had thrown in to surprise them? But the rope was leaning heavily toward the other side as JoJo's team tried hard to hang on. The other team did not seem to be facing the same sort of trouble JoJo's team was. JoJo dug her fingers into the coils of the rope and gritted her teeth, leaning backward in an attempt to reset the balance. She looked across the rope at Belle, who was grinning as she tugged.

JoJo frowned. Did Belle have something to do with this? But how? Then she remembered: Belle had left breakfast early to go to the bathroom. She definitely could have grabbed oil from the kitchen and slicked up the rope. JoJo leaned all her weight backward, and for a minute, she thought her side was gaining traction. But then she heard a loud yelp as one of the girls behind her slipped and landed with a plop on the ground. Then Belle's team gave one last, hard tug, and JoJo's side moved about three feet forward as they went down.

Straight into the mud.

"Huh?" JoJo looked at her palms and met Miley's eyes. Miley's knees were covered in mud, and JoJo's hands were sopping. The ground beneath her a minute ago had been dry, but the ground between the teams had apparently been soft and muddy, something JoJo only just figured out . . . as she was lying in it!

"That's weird," Bethany said, looking quizzically at them. "Girls—I don't know—can someone tell me how the ground got so muddy?" She touched it with her sneaker-clad toe as JoJo's team began to pick themselves up and wipe off the mud as best they could.

"It's almost as if someone dumped a bucket of water here just before we started!" Her eyebrows squished together as she tried to figure it out.

"And the rope was oily," said one of the girls from JoJo's team.

Bethany reached for the rope and felt it for herself. Her look of confusion deepened into a frown.

"Girls," she said, "I will not make any accusations. But whomever did this was very wrong. It is *never* funny to cheat. Does anyone know how this happened?"

Everyone looked at each other, then shook their heads. JoJo gave Belle a long look, but Belle's face was the picture of innocence.

"Well," Bethany said finally, "I can't do anything without knowing who the culprit is." She shook her head. "There's no victory in winning when you weren't all on equal

47

footing," she told Belle's team. "I declare it a draw. You will *all* help clean up after dinner tonight. And we won't have any more contests. I want you to make friends this weekend, not rivals." Belle groaned loudly, but Bethany ignored her. "Now go get cleaned up," Bethany said to JoJo's group. "We're meeting in front of the stables in half an hour for horseback riding."

"I miss Dusty so much!" Miley exclaimed as they approached a fenced-in pasture where three horses were grazing. The girls were spotless, having jumped in the showers before changing. "I'm going to go straight to the stables when I get home tomorrow night." Miley loved her pet pony so much and visited her at the stables where Dusty lived every chance she got. Sometimes Dusty even got to visit Miley in her backyard!

"I miss BowBow too," JoJo agreed, thinking of her sweet little Yorkie. She never traveled without BowBow—this was a first. BowBow even flew on planes! But then, BowBow wasn't exactly the camping type, JoJo reminded herself. She probably wouldn't have enjoyed the rustic vibe of the weekend.

"We ride horses at our aunt and uncle's ranch in Texas," Reagan told Miley and JoJo as she and Sydney each grabbed a handful of baby carrots from the bucket by the fence and began offering them to the horses.

"That's so cool!" JoJo exclaimed. "Then you two must be pros. You can show us the ropes."

"The groom should be here in a minute to help us get started," Jamilla told them. "I'm so excited! I haven't ridden a horse myself since I was an Art Star!"

"It's a piece of cake," Belle said, approaching their group with her campers in tow. "At least, if you're an animal person. Animals love me." She turned to her group and said, "We've got this, right, Queen Bs?" Her campers cheered, but one or two sounded a little half-hearted, JoJo thought. "We're going to win!" Belle went on.

By then Bahi and her campers had joined them. "Belle," Bahi said with a laugh, "it isn't a contest!"

"Everything in life is a contest," Belle said. She smirked as though she was joking, but JoJo thought she looked a little serious. Belle's campers looked scared.

"Not if you're the only ones competing," Jamilla said lightly. "Our group is here to have fun!" When Belle wasn't looking, she winked at Belle's camper Madeleine, who gave her a grateful smile. Just then, a very tall woman with long, dark hair tied in a long braid stepped out of the stables.

"Welcome, Art Stars!" she said, clapping for their attention. "Today we're going to spend a little time learning how to groom and ride horses." JoJo saw Belle roll her eyes and begin to fiddle with her phone while the woman began telling them the ins and outs of brushing a horse's hair and cleaning their hooves. Finally, the woman did a demonstration on how to saddle a horse. Belle's nose was still buried in her phone. Which reminded JoJo: She was going to have to visit the main office and use her own phone to call her mom later and give her updates! But for now, JoJo was paying attention. She'd never groomed or ridden a horse before, and she wanted to know the difference between a curry comb and a hoof pick. Jamilla was listening closely too, but JoJo saw Bahi watching Belle with worried eyes.

Finally, it was time to begin brushing their

horses. JoJo and Miley were put in charge of a dapper, brown-and-white-spotted horse named Macaroni (because she loved to snack on pasta). Miley pulled on a grooming mitt, and JoJo started with a mane and tail brush, working her way through Macaroni's beautiful brown mane. Macaroni knickered, and Jamilla, who was overseeing the girls' work, offered her a carrot. "Sorry it's not pasta, Macaroni!" Jamilla giggled as the horse gently nibbled at the carrot.

Finally, it was time for the girls to ride. A riding instructor helped Sydney and Reagan get seated together atop a horse named Starflash, and Miley was seated on Macaroni after getting a big boost up from Jamilla and JoJo. JoJo was excited to ride next but was even more excited to watch her friend trot Macaroni! They had been instructed to go in a circle around the fenced-in pasture. The instructor had shown them how to let the horses know they wanted to turn left or right, as well as go fast or slow. "These horses won't go too fast, though!" she assured them.

"I *want* to go fast," Belle announced from atop Sprout, her large black mare.

The instructor laughed. "These horses are the lazy ones," she told her. "They know their job is to enjoy a slow stroll. They'll set the pace—you'll see." JoJo could tell the instructor's words didn't sit well with Belle, who frowned. And JoJo also knew Belle wasn't one to back down from a challenge. She just hoped Belle would set a good example for her campers and take everyone's safety seriously.

As soon as the instructor gave the go-ahead, all the campers kicked off. Everyone was having fun. A little blond camper on a brown pony couldn't stop giggling.

Sydney and Reagan were trotting around in circles—but tiny ones, not a big enclosed circle like everyone else—and cracking up. "I'm getting dizzy!" shouted Sydney. The instructor stepped in to lead them back on track—Starflash had been chasing a fly on her tail!

"I can't wait for our turn," said Bahi, who stood by JoJo, taking it all in. "I was afraid of horses as a kid, I think just because of how big they are. But these ones are so gentle! I'm excited to give it a shot. And Belle was super excited too. She loves animals," Bahi said.

"I didn't know that," said JoJo. "How long have you two been friends, anyway?"

"Since we were little kids," Bahi replied. "Belle was my first friend in dance class when I was four! I was so nervous and shy, and she really took me under her wing and made me feel included."

"That's so great," JoJo said. "I can see why you're such close friends."

Bahi looked thoughtful. "We don't always agree on things now," she started, watching Belle work her way around the circle. "And Belle has her moments. But she's a good and loyal friend deep down. And loyalty is really important to me."

"I get it 100 percent," JoJo said. "I feel the same way about Miley." She was glad Bahi had opened up to her—and glad she could understand Bahi's friendship with Belle a little better now, so she could look for the good in Belle.

Just then, they heard a shriek from the circle of trotting horses. Belle was galloping her horse around the others—much faster than they were supposed to go. She'd just zipped within an inch of Jamilla, who clearly wasn't expecting it. Jamilla swayed a bit on top of her horse, then regained her balance. For a minute, it had looked as if she was going to fall!

"Faster, faster, yeehaw!" Belle was yelling into the horse's ear while moving the reins up and down rapidly.

"Stop!" cried the instructor. "The horses don't like to be pushed like that!"

Belle ignored her and zipped faster and faster around the enclosure. Meanwhile, Macaroni, with Miley on top of her, had stopped moving entirely—clearly the other horses weren't used to all the drama! The instructor dashed after Sprout and Belle, but it was looking hopeless, and Sprout was starting to zigzag from side to side—way too close to the other horses for it to be safe.

JoJo had an idea. She put two fingers in her mouth and let out a loud, piercing whistle. Sprout skidded to a halt, nearly bucking

Belle—but Belle held tight. The instructor approached the horse, who was still shaking his head as if upset, and offered him a carrot, soothing him. Sprout gradually calmed down, but Belle glared at JoJo.

"I'm going to have to speak with Bethany about this," the instructor said. "As a counselor, Belle, you're supposed to be setting a good example for the campers. Forcing Sprout into a gallop was against the rules."

Bahi clutched JoJo's hand. "Oh, I hope she apologizes," she whispered.

"Sorry," Belle finally said, smiling at the instructor. To her credit, she did look sorry. "I didn't realize I was scaring the other riders. I was just having so much fun."

The instructor's face softened. "It's easy to get carried away," she remarked. "Just don't do it again." Bahi's grip on JoJo's hand relaxed.

"One more lap," the instructor said to the

riders. "Come on, giddyap." She patted Macaroni on her flank to get her moving again.

Half an hour later, JoJo and Bahi and a few other campers finished up their rides—JoJo on Sprout, who was sweet and easy for her—and the group headed to the lake for a kayaking lesson. After that, they'd have lunch, followed by a hike and dinner and another campfire. Aside from the obvious drama, JoJo was loving being in the great outdoors. JoJo and Jamilla shared a kayak, and JoJo had never had more fun in her life . . . even when their kayak capsized!

"Snake!" Jamilla shrieked when they were halfway out in the lake. Sure enough, there was a tiny green snake near her seat. Jamilla stood up, and the whole kayak rocked.

"Sit down," JoJo told her friend—but Jamilla was *really* scared of reptiles, so not only did she stand up, she leaned to the side of the kayak! The boat tipped over, and both girls fell out. Luckily, they were wearing life vests. When they bobbed to the surface of the water and, with the help of the lifeguard, righted their kayak and climbed back in, JoJo noticed a piece of green plastic partially lodged into the paddle holder.

"Wait a sec—Jamilla, is this the snake you were afraid of?" JoJo held the fake plastic snake in her palm.

"Oh my gosh. JoJo, I thought it was the real thing!" Jamilla clapped her hands over her mouth. "You've got to be kidding me. But how—?"

"Oh, I think I know how," JoJo said grimly, glancing over at Bahi and Belle in their kayak. Belle was cracking up—laughing so hard she kept wiping tears from her eyes. Bahi mouthed, "Sorry," to Jamilla and JoJo.

"Cut it out," JoJo heard Bahi tell her friend.

"Oh, I'm just playing around," Belle responded.

But Jamilla and JoJo were *not* laughing.

They also did not laugh during lunch, when the salt and sugar shakers were mixed up and their lids loosened so JoJo poured a mound of sugar on her french fries by mistake.

And they *definitely* did not laugh when they came back to their cabin after lunch to change for their hike . . . and found bunches of wriggly earthworms in their beds!

Was Belle aiming to be the best at pranks now? JoJo wondered. Because if so, she was definitely winning!

"This is out of control," Miley said, as Sydney and Reagan jumped around, screaming.

"Here, I'll take them outside," Jamilla assured her campers. "I don't mind worms." She grabbed a plastic cup from the bathroom and scooped all the creepy crawlies from the girls' pillows to the cup, then calmly carried it outside and dumped it. By the time Jamilla returned, JoJo and Miley were already deep in conversation.

"I think this means war," Miley said grimly. "These pranks are just a step too far."

"No way," JoJo said. "Siwanatorz never bully back. You know that! We're just going to be good sports and keep on having fun. Besides, is it just me, or are sugary french fries kind of great?"

"But, JoJo, if I wake up with worms on my pillow, I'll freak," Sydney complained.

"We'll make sure nothing bad happens to you," Jamilla assured her little camper. "Belle might be messing with us for laughs, but she doesn't want to hurt us. And if this sort of thing continues to happen, I can always talk to Bethany about it."

"Yeah. And I've got the best fix for slimy, gross, wriggly worms right here," Miley told them. She reached into her backpack and pulled out a giant bag of . . . gummy worms! "I never travel without 'em," she said, laughing.

So when Belle popped her head in a few minutes later to "say hi and check in," instead of finding a bunch of girls freaking out over earthworms, she found a bunch of girls cracking up together and snacking on gummy worms.

"Care for a worm?" Miley held out the open bag with a big smile, and Belle's jaw dropped. JoJo couldn't help but giggle. Miley was a real Siwanator—and this time, being the bigger person felt extra sweet.

CHAPTER 4

A few minutes later, the girls in JoJo's cabin pulled on their hiking boots and filled their water bottles in the bathroom sink. Jamilla packed a bag full of granola bars and trail mix. Then they joined the other campers near the lake to meet Bethany, who was going to be their guide. When they got there, JoJo couldn't help but notice that Belle had on flip-flops, not sneakers. She also wasn't wearing her Art Stars T-shirt. Her campers, at least, seemed dressed for the hike with layers and sneakers.

"A few guidelines before we get moving," Bethany said. "First off: We only hike as fast as the slowest member of our group. That means no going off alone, no matter how excited you are. Second," she continued, "if you're in trouble or lost, stay put and blow on this whistle"—she began handing out colorful whistles to the group—"until one of the counselors or I come to find you. Third, if you see a wild animal or insect, don't mess with it. Most critters like to be left alone, and that includes honeybees. So even if you see an animal that scares you, don't panic. These trails are easy and calm—we aren't going very far into the wilderness."

JoJo was distracted by the sound of Belle's voice coming from her left. She looked over to see Belle whispering to Bahi, who seemed like she was trying to listen to Bethany but having a hard time. When Bethany handed the girls their whistles, Belle barely noticed. She absently shoved it in to her back pocket.

"Finally, drink plenty of water," Bethany went on. "It's important to stay hydrated!"

The girls all nodded, and Bethany tossed an orange tee to Belle, who scowled. "You're going to want to wear this so your campers can spot you," she said. Belle reluctantly pulled it on over her tank.

"Queen Bs, here we go!" shouted Belle to her campers. Then they broke into a song they'd clearly practiced. But at least they were having fun! One little girl with red hair and a tiara was pouring her heart into it.

"Who's in the house?" Belle chanted.

"Queen Bs in the house," her campers responded.

"Who's number one?"

"Queen Bs are number one!"

"Who's—"

"Belle," JoJo heard Bethany say gently, "we're all on the same team here. Now let's get moving, okay?"

"If anyone should be Queen 'Bee,' it's Bethany," Miley said quietly to JoJo as they began to hike the gently sloping path ahead. "She's the adult in charge."

"Belle's really great most of the time," Bahi said, hopping over a jagged stone in the path to join them. JoJo cringed—she hadn't realized Bahi had heard Miley's words. Even though Miley wasn't saying anything mean, she hoped Bahi didn't feel bad.

"Bahi, I'm sorry," Miley said sincerely, her forehead crinkling. "I only meant that 'Bethany' begins with a 'B' and she's the adult, so . . ."

"That's okay," Bahi told her. She glanced

at her friend, who was several yards ahead, encouraging her campers to keep up. "It's just that I see so many great things about her, and I wish you could see them too. In groups she gets nervous, I think. One-on-one, she's funny and loyal. She'd stick up for me anytime—she *has*. One time when we were little, we were running relay races and my overalls fell down! They fell *all the way down*," Bahi said in a hushed tone, then shuddered for good measure. "I burst into tears! It was SO embarrassing. But Belle started making chicken noises and running in circles saying 'bawk bawk bawk' to distract all the other kids until I picked myself up and stopped crying. By the time I was ready to play again, they'd all forgotten what had happened in the first place."

"Wow," JoJo said. "That's really nice."

"Yeah. I know she can be a lot sometimes. But she's my best friend," Bahi explained, tucking a loose strand of black hair behind her ear. "And I love her."

"I totally get it," JoJo said.

"Me too," said Miley. "I just wish we could see that side of her more often."

"Her campers are really starting to love her too," Bahi told them. "It was a rocky start, but Belle is so much fun, and I really think she's bonding with them."

Just then, Belle ran up to them. She leaned in and tickled Bahi's armpit, and Bahi squealed and jumped. "Come on, Bahi," Belle said to her friend. "At the very top of this slope is an amazing view. Bethany's already there." The two ran ahead.

A few paces in front of Miley and JoJo was Jamilla, who was keeping all the younger campers in line. "Don't go off the path," JoJo heard Jamilla call toward Sydney and

Reagan, who were holding hands and dashing through the trees.

A few minutes later, JoJo and Miley reached the clearing Belle had been talking about. Bethany was waiting for them with snacks, and some of the campers were sitting cross-legged and staring out at the late-afternoon sun and the view of the lake below.

"Look, it's our dock!" Jamilla exclaimed.

"And that's where our kayak tipped," giggled JoJo, breaking into a granola bar.

Bethany took out her phone and snapped a bunch of photos of the campers at the peak. "These will go into our slideshow for after the talent show," she promised. JoJo realized she hadn't missed her own phone once since they'd arrived. She had called her mom during lunch that day, and that was enough for her. But she *was* glad Bethany had captured the moment.

"What do you think's down that trail?" Belle asked, pointing in the opposite direction from where they'd come.

"We're not going to find out," Bethany told her. "It's for very advanced hikers only. We're going back the way we came." Belle nodded, but JoJo thought she saw a dangerous glint in her eye.

"Let's pack up," Bethany told the group. "We need to make sure we get back to camp before sunset." She straightened and slung her backpack over her shoulders, then began to count the campers.

"Counselors, take inventory of your bunks," she instructed.

Just then, JoJo heard a shriek. "Bees!" Belle screamed, jumping up and down and clutching her shoulder. For a second, JoJo thought she was talking to her campers, the Queen Bs. Then she turned around and saw Belle swatting at the air—exactly what Bethany had told them *not* to do if they saw a bee, back when Belle wasn't listening.

Suddenly all the campers were yelling and running around, thrashing at the air around them. JoJo didn't even see any bees! But she knew this was *not* okay. She and Miley looked at each other. "Miley, you grab Sydney and Reagan," she told her friend. "I'll help Jamilla with Belle's campers."

Bethany was blowing her whistle. "Calm down, everyone!" she yelled. "Get in a single-file line!" The whistle only seemed to make everyone more panicked. One freckled girl with long blond hair and bangs was crying, and a couple of the others were wandering around, looking confused. JoJo wasn't afraid of bees. She had been stung before, but she

71

wasn't allergic. And if there was a hive, there would have been a swarm by now. But the air around them was clear and still.

It was only when all the campers were lined up single file and heading back down toward the bunks that JoJo remembered: Belle was *really* good at making a scene—Bahi had told them as much.

Good enough to fake a bee sighting?

CHAPTER 5

"Sixteen, seventeen, eighteen . . ." Bethany bit the bottom of her lip and started counting the group again, looking worried. "One, two, three . . ." she started, tapping each girl's head as she went down the line. The sun was starting to set, and the sky was lit up orange and pink. "Campers, please take a look around and make sure all of your bunk-mates are here," Bethany said in a steady voice. "Did anyone go to the bathroom or leave already for their bunk?"

JoJo looked around. Jamilla was there, and Miley was next to her, scuffing the ground with her shoe. Sydney and Reagan were seated in the grass by the base of the trail, drinking from their matching pink water bottles. Their glow-in-the-dark necklaces were beginning to shine green in the waning light. JoJo spotted Bahi with her group. Bahi was counting her campers—all four were there. JoJo saw panic cross Bahi's face. Then Bahi took off toward the bunks.

All at once, JoJo realized who was missing.

"Miley, it's Belle! Belle isn't here," JoJo whispered to her friend.

"Maybe she just went back to the bunks? She's not very good at listening," Miley pointed out. But Bahi was already emerging from Belle's bunk with a scared look on her face. Bahi went straight to Bethany. JoJo, Miley, and Jamilla were close enough to hear the conversation.

"Belle is missing," Bahi said.

"Okay," Bethany replied. "When did you last see her?"

"When she was swatting away the bees," Bahi said. The other girls nodded to confirm that that was when they had also seen Belle last.

"Well she isn't allergic to bees," Bethany mused aloud.

"That's right," Bahi responded. "At least, I don't think she is. I guess I've never seen her get stung, and we haven't talked about it."

"It wasn't listed on her allergy checklist," Bethany said. "Otherwise we'd have been prepared. I'm sure she's okay, Bahi. It's very safe here, and our trail was meant for beginners."

"I'm really scared of bees," Bahi confessed,

a tear running down her cheek. "That's why I left so fast and didn't check to see if Belle was with me."

"Bahi, do you have any idea where Belle might have gone?" Bethany wanted to know. "She can't be lost, or she'd have blown her whistle for us to find her."

"I don't think she heard you say that, about the whistles," Miley told Bethany quietly. "She wasn't paying attention."

"Oy." Bethany sighed. "Okay. All of you know Belle, right? Let's quickly usher the other campers back to the party barn. Jamilla," she said to the older girl, "will you stay with them? It's time for pizza, and you can put on a movie to keep them occupied. The rest of us will put our heads together."

Jamilla nodded and began herding the kids toward the party barn. They followed her eagerly. JoJo felt her own stomach growl—they were all probably starving after that long hike.

Now it was just JoJo, Bahi, and Miley left at the campsite with Bethany.

"Bahi, you're closest to Belle," Bethany said. "Do you have any idea where she might have gone?" Bahi shook her head, looking upset. Tears were forming in the corners of her eyes.

"I might," JoJo said. She was nervous to tell Bethany what she thought—she didn't want to get Belle in trouble. But it was getting darker, and Belle's safety was important. She knew she shouldn't keep her mouth shut when she might be able to help, even if Belle might be mad later.

"She was really into that other trail," JoJo said. "The one you said was for advanced hikers."

Bahi's eyes widened. "Belle really does not

like being told 'no,'" she said. "And she loves a challenge. Do you think . . . ?"

"Did anyone see a bee?" JoJo asked softly. "I didn't."

Miley shook her head. "I didn't either."

"I actually didn't," Bethany said grimly. Bahi looked close to tears, and also angry.

"You think she distracted us so she could take the other path?" Bahi asked JoJo.

"I think it's worth a look," JoJo said.

Bethany was looking more and more worried as the sun sank behind the mountaintop. "I'm going to call the forest patrol for backup," she told the girls. "There's nothing for you to do now. We'll send out a search party along both hiking trails. Hopefully she didn't stray far."

"Can't we help?" JoJo wanted to know.

"It's too dark for you to help with the search, but you can help by watching a movie with the other campers," Bethany said. "Bahi, you, Jamilla, Margot, and the other five counselors are in charge. Please round them up. I am hoping this is all an accident, because if Belle wandered off on purpose, that's a very bad thing." Bethany's lips were pursed. "She was supposed to be looking after her campers," she said. "Going off on her own is very wrong, if that's what happened."

JoJo nodded, then wrapped one arm around Bahi's shoulders and another around Miley's and led them back toward the party barn. Once they were settled in beanbags in the back of the group, with *Harriet the Spy* playing on the projector screen ahead and heaping plates of pepperoni pizza in hand, everyone began to feel a little better.

"Belle is really strong and fearless," Bahi reassured them. "She can handle anything. And she isn't afraid of the dark. She'll be okay." Bahi sounded confident, but she was chewing on a strand of her hair and hadn't touched her pizza.

"She'll be okay, Bahi." Miley reached out and squeezed the other girl's hand.

"Shhhh!" someone said from a beanbag up front.

"Belle's like Harriet," JoJo whispered. "She's a trailblazer."

Bahi nodded in agreement. "A literal *trail-blazer*," she said, smiling a little. Then she hesitated. "I want her to be okay," Bahi told them. "But I'm also really mad she did this."

"We don't know for sure what happened," JoJo said. "We should let Belle speak for herself when she's back." But privately, she agreed. If Belle invented the bees to cause a distraction so she could slip away unseen, it would be a lie, and unfair to everyone who was worried about her.

Jamilla brought out tubs of ice cream just then, and one of the other counselors—a friendly girl with a sparkling blue eyes who had introduced herself as Samantha—paused the movie.

"Dessert break!" she said, beginning to toss out empty pizza boxes and laying out the ice cream and toppings on the table along one wall of the barn where the pizza had been. Everyone jumped to their feet and formed a line with Jamilla and Bahi's help. If there was one thing JoJo loved, it was an ice cream bar!

"Thanks, girl," she told Jamilla, who gave her a giant scoop of chocolate ice cream. "You're doing a great job of holding down the fort and keeping everyone happy."

"I love sleepovers," Jamilla told her. "Camp is just one big sleepover in the woods. And what's a sleepover without a sundae bar?"

The girls settled back into their beanbags

to watch the movie, which was almost over. As the credits began to roll, a camper in front of JoJo took a bite of her ice cream, then yawned. It felt awfully quiet there without Belle's usual tricks, JoJo realized. And it was only eight o'clock! As much as Belle could be a pain, JoJo sort of missed the random fun she brought to camp. Sure, the fake snake trick hadn't been nice. And the worms had been squirmy, wormy, *gross*. But both incidents had ended in laughter. JoJo didn't like the surprise element of things . . . but wasn't camp about having fun and letting loose? JoJo looked at Miley, and Miley looked at JoJo, and because they were *that* close, JoJo could tell Miley was thinking the same thing.

Miley got a devilish gleam in her eye. She dug her plastic spoon into the mound of whipped cream on top of her ice cream. She angled the whipped cream–filled spoon back with one finger while keeping the other end steady with the opposite hand. Then she let her finger go and sent the whipped cream sailing through the air. It landed with a splat on the arm of a small, dark-skinned girl with bangs.

"Hey!" She leapt to her feet. "What do you think you're doing?" Then she licked the whipped cream right off her arm and giggled. "Mmm," she said. The girl looked at the sundae bar. She looked at Miley, who reached back for another dollop of whipped cream. And the girl dashed over to the sundae bar, sticking her hand right into the bowl of sprinkles and tossed them over their heads like confetti. "Party time!" she shouted.

"Uh-oh," Bahi said.

"Is this a party barn or what?" JoJo countered. She figured Bethany might not be thrilled . . . but sometimes it was okay to take a page from Belle's book, as long as they stayed safe. Bahi shrugged and smiled, then stood up, nearly getting hit by a stray blob of ice cream. She dusted off her hands on her jeans, then dashed to the sundae bar and grabbed a can of whipped cream, shooting it off into the crowd. Girls were sticky and giggling now, laughing as they sent ice cream flying through the room.

Everyone was messy. Everyone was breaking the rules. Everyone was *definitely* having fun. *Mission accomplished,* thought JoJo.

CHAPTER 6

When Bethany came back, Miley and JoJo were beginning to clean up the mess in the party barn and Bahi, Jamilla, and the other counselors had started to herd the other campers to the showers to get cleaned up. JoJo knew from the look on Bethany's face that the news was not good. And Bethany's frown only deepened when she took in the damage around her.

"What on earth happened?" she wanted to know.

"Ice cream fight," Miley explained. Bethany's eyes widened, but then she shrugged and waved them off. "I can't even touch that," she said, sinking into a chair next to the cartons of melting ice cream.

"Did you . . . Is Belle still lost?" JoJo wanted to know. She felt worried. She had been sure Bethany would return with a laughing Belle in tow.

"She is," Bethany confirmed. "The forest patrol combed both paths just to cover all bases, but she's nowhere to be found." Bethany took out her phone and began to fiddle with it. "The police are on their way," she explained. "Girls, thank you for your help today. While we're waiting for the police to arrive, let's get this mess cleaned up and get everyone safely into their bunks."

JoJo stared at Bethany's phone. She had a funny feeling, like there was something at the back of her mind . . . something she couldn't quite remember . . .

"I've got it!" JoJo shouted. "Belle has her cell phone with her. We can track her!"

"She has her cell phone?" Bethany frowned.

"Yes—she didn't turn it in. I saw her using it to take selfies while we were hiking."

"Good thinking, JoJo," Bethany said. "Maybe overlooking the rules will work in Belle's favor this once!"

"But wouldn't she have called us already?" Miley wanted to know. "I bet you there's no signal up there. She would have at least called Bahi or her mom, even if she didn't have our numbers."

"Bahi's phone is in the admin office with ours," JoJo reminded her.

"I'll hunt down Belle's phone number and give it a try," Bethany told the girls. "Even if we can't reach her, hopefully her phone had a signal at some point on the mountain. I noticed mine still had a signal when I took it out to snap photos—we didn't go high enough to lose it completely throughout the whole hike. Even if we can get a general read on her location when her phone last had a signal, that's a start. Now go get cleaned up and ready for bed," Bethany told them. "I'll let everyone know as soon as Belle is back safe and sound."

By the time the girls finished cleaning up the party barn and headed back to their bunks, they were exhausted. JoJo worried about Bahi, who was in her own cabin, but Jamilla assured her that Bahi was staying strong. Since Belle wasn't overseeing her campers, they were divided between the two closest cabins, so everyone could have a buddy in their new cabin. Since Jamilla's cabin was right next to Belle's, two extra campers had joined the party. JoJo and Miley had offered to share a bed so everyone else could have her own space. JoJo and Miley would be tight as sardines in their bunk bed—they didn't mind, but the new arrangement meant word of Belle's disappearance had gotten out. Jamilla was trying to get them all to settle down, but the girls were hyped up on sugar and nerves.

"I bet she got eaten by a bear," Madeleine said, tossing her blond hair over one shoulder. "There are all kinds of wild animals out there."

"Mads, come on," Liz said. Her striking green eyes rolled in the semi-dark. JoJo had met Liz before on the dance scene—she was one of the best young dancers JoJo had seen.

Almost guaranteed to go pro. She was also a fan favorite for her sassy stage presence. "Don't be silly," she went on. "I bet you the ghost of Tim Crowley got her."

"What?!" Sydney shrieked. "A ghost? What ghost?"

"Who is Tim Crowley?" Reagan echoed, looking freaked out.

JoJo wished Liz hadn't gone there.

"Tim Crowley is a nine-foot-tall lepre-chaun," Liz started.

"*What?*" Sydney shrieked again, and this time JoJo laughed.

"I thought leprechauns were short?" Miley wanted to know.

"They can be any size. They're pretend," clarified Liz.

"There is no ghost!" Jamilla cut in. "Girls! Settle down. We may as well try and get some sleep."

On the one hand, JoJo didn't think it was nice to be joking around about a ghost snatching Belle. On the other hand, she was glad the other campers didn't seem all that worried or scared. It was better that way. She snuggled under her own sleeping bag and tried to get comfortable as Jamilla turned out the lights.

"Can we sing our goodnight song?" Madeleine wanted to know. "Belle sang it with us last night."

"Sure," Jamilla told her. "How does it go?"

"Give me a B!" Madeleine started, and JoJo cringed a little. *Another Queen Bs thing,* she thought.

"B!" yelled Liz.

"You've got the beat, you've got the beat," Madeleine continued, and JoJo saw that she was wrong. Then Liz chimed in, and JoJo could see they were really enjoying the cheer Belle had taught them. Just as they quieted down, Liz spoke up.

"I really miss Belle," she said. "I hope she's okay."

"Should we put good wishes into the night for her?" Jamilla asked.

"How do you do that?" Miley wanted to know. Suddenly the cabin was quiet as all the girls waited to hear what Jamilla would say.

"You look out that window, find a star, and make a wish," Jamilla explained. "Then you take a deep breath, close your eyes, and picture an envelope. You put your wish inside the envelope and, *woosh*, send it to Belle. Easy peasy."

"There are a million stars!"

"So we'll give Belle a million wishes," Jamilla said. "Let's get started."

At that, all the campers went quiet, sending Belle their wishes. JoJo was willing to

92

bet all the wishes were mostly the same. *We wish you're safe. We wish you'll come back soon.* They wished their wishes silently until they started to drop off to sleep one by one.

CHAPTER 7

"Give me a B," JoJo heard, and she thought she was dreaming of the night before. Then she shot up in bed and whacked her head on the bunk above her. Beside her, Miley yawned and stretched noisily.

"Ow," JoJo muttered, rubbing her forehead.

"Give me a B," the voice said, louder, and this time JoJo knew she wasn't dreaming.

"Belle?" she asked, jumping out of bed.

"Queen B in the house!" Belle shouted, and

JoJo couldn't even be annoyed because she was so glad Belle was back safe and sound. Belle was standing in the doorway of their cabin, balanced on a pair of crutches. Bethany and Bahi stood behind her, smiling.

"Belle, you're safe!" her campers squealed, swarming around her and smothering her with hugs.

"Watch the leg, ladies!" Belle warned, but she was smiling. "And by 'Queen B' I meant Bethany, by the way. She totally saved my life."

"Well, I wouldn't go that far," Bethany said. "And besides, it was JoJo who had the idea."

"What happened?" Miley asked.

"JoJo, thank you," Belle said, sounding sincere. "I'll tell you both the whole story later. For now, I hear our campers have some practicing to do for the talent show." Everyone cheered, but Bethany cleared her throat.

"Belle, we haven't really had a chance to talk since last night," she said. "Why don't you come with me to the admin office? We'll meet the others at breakfast."

In the party barn a little while later, JoJo and Miley were loading up on seconds of scrambled eggs and bacon—and Bahi and Madeleine were heaping their plates with waffles and strawberries since they were both vegetarian—when Belle appeared. Madeleine went off to sit with Liz, Sydney, Reagan, Samantha, and Margot—leaving JoJo, Bahi, Jamilla, Miley, and Belle alone at a long picnic table. Bahi stood up to fix a plate for Belle, who was clearly starving, since she ate the waffle Bahi gave her in practically one bite.

"I owe all of you an apology," Belle said, when everyone was seated with their plates and Belle's crutches. "I honestly didn't mean to be gone half the night. But I worried you all, and I broke the rules. And I scared everyone. There *was* a bee," she went on, "but just a little one, and it didn't sting me. I freaked out about it because I wanted to distract everyone so I could try the advanced path, at least for a few minutes. I planned to just walk down a little bit and then catch up with you guys on the other path."

"Why would you do that, Belle?" Bahi looked upset. "We were so worried. And you were supposed to be looking after your campers."

"I know," Belle said. "And I also am the person who ruined tug-of-war," she confessed. "It's never good to break the rules, and I really am sorry. I just feel like . . ." She trailed off. "Sometimes I feel like I don't fit in. So I act a little wild for attention."

"We all really like you, Belle," Miley said,

her voice kind. "We want to be your friend. But it's hard when you have to be the best at everything, especially when you do it by cutting us down or playing tricks."

Belle's lower lip trembled. "I know," she said. "I don't know what to say. I don't deserve a second chance, but I'd really like one. JoJo"—she turned to JoJo, looking her in the eye—"Bethany told me what you did. That you remembered I had my phone. And that you figured I might have gone down the other path. Well, when I went down the advanced path, I veered from the main trail and fell down. It was super steep, and I couldn't keep a good grip with my flip-flops on. My phone had a signal but I lost it—it flew off the side of the slope and landed who knows where. I couldn't look for it, because I couldn't walk. But Bethany tracked it, and then she could hear me shouting for help. The forest patrol carried me down on a stretcher. But if it weren't for you, I might have been there all night long. It was cold and really scary. I'm just grateful you guys cared enough to help, especially after how I was acting."

"Of course I wanted to help," JoJo told Belle. "That's what Siwanatorz do. And, Belle, sometimes your pranks aren't funny . . . but you are super fun. Your campers adore you! I think if you followed the rules and didn't always try to be number one, you'd be a great counselor."

"And a great friend," Miley piped in.

"You already are," Bahi said. "At least to me!"

"Hey, I want in on this," Jamilla said. "After all, we have history!"

"Way back to dance workshop," Belle agreed. "When JoJo saved the day *again*." Her smile at JoJo was full and genuine. "I don't know about you all"—she nodded at Jamilla, Bahi, and Miley—"but I consider myself a Siwanator for life!"

JoJo laughed and blushed. "I really didn't do anything this time," she said. "Except help start an epic food fight."

"What?" Belle gasped. "No way! What did I miss?!" Then she got that familiar, devilish glint in her eye. "Food fight, eh . . ." She stared down at her food.

"Belle, you've been on solid ground with Bethany for about five seconds!" Bahi laughed. "Don't mess it up!"

"Okay, okay," Belle agreed, smiling.

"Anyway, we have to get practicing! The talent show is this afternoon," JoJo reminded her. "And a lot of parents will be there."

Belle's face darkened. "I actually . . . I won't be participating," she told them. "My campers will, but Bethany said I'm disqualified for my behavior."

"Oh no!" Miley said. "You were looking forward to it so much!"

"You've been invested in the talent show from day one!" Jamilla added. "You even tried to make it into a contest," she teased. "That is true dedication. You have to perform!"

"I screwed up." Belle shrugged. "In a pretty big way. I guess I deserve it. And anyway, I'm on crutches, so I can't dance."

"No way," JoJo said. "No Siwanator is missing out on the talent show on my watch. And besides," she said thoughtfully, "you weren't the only one to break the rules. Just let me handle this. And get practicing—because if I know anything, it's that dancing is definitely not your only talent!"

Belle laughed. "Well, I'm pretty good at a few other things," she agreed. "I'm the absolute best at . . ."

All the girls groaned. And Miley flung some whipped cream from her waffle straight at Belle—it went *splat* on her forehead.

Belle's mouth hung open in shock.

"Well, you said you didn't want to miss out," Miley said with a shrug.

At that, Belle grinned wider than she had all weekend.

CHAPTER 8

"In conclusion," JoJo said from where she sat in the admin office, "if Belle is disqualified from the talent show for breaking the rules, we *all* have to be disqualified, because we all broke the rules during our food fight yesterday."

Bethany smiled and shook her head. "JoJo, you really know how to make a point," she said, laughing. "We certainly can't lose all our extremely talented campers from the talent show—the parents are looking forward to it! But you're right that you broke the rules too, and I have to be consistent." She paused, as if lost in thought. "Okay," Bethany said, twirling a pencil on her fingertips. "Here's the deal. You can all—including Belle—take part in the talent show *if* you work together."

"You mean no individual performances?" JoJo wanted to know.

"No . . . there can still be individual performances for some campers," Bethany explained. "But I'd like Belle to demonstrate that she can work with a group. I think it's very important for her development as a dancer. So I'd like you and Belle and anyone else you'd like to include to co-plan your performances. That way you can be as silly as you want to be and not worry about outperforming each other."

"Okay!" JoJo leaned forward in her chair,

enthusiastic. "That sounds great. Sometimes we're so focused on winning that we forget the reasons why we all got into dancing and singing and choreographing in the first place. Because it's fun, and we love it!"

Bethany smiled at JoJo's enthusiasm, but then her expression turned serious. "I do want you to know that there will be serious consequences for Belle, JoJo, even though she gets to perform in the talent show. Her antics weren't all fun—some were dangerous, and others were disrespectful. Her behavior was inappropriate, especially when she was meant to be acting as a mentor to you girls. She and I will be having a conversation about it with her parents. But I'm glad you came to speak with me about the talent show. I think it's a good idea to include her in the weekend's closing event."

JoJo nodded. "Thanks, Bethany." She

wondered what the consequences would be but figured Belle would share with her if she was comfortable.

"Well then," Bethany said. "Go spread the word about the talent show! You have all afternoon to work together to create a fun performance for the parents to watch. They're arriving at 4 P.M."

JoJo thanked Bethany and headed back to her bunk, excited to share the news. As a group, with all their talents combined, the possibilities for their routine were endless! When she burst through the entrance to the cabin, it was chaos. There was clothing *everywhere*. And Belle was there with her girls, as was Bahi.

"What are you guys doing?" JoJo exclaimed.

"We're improvising costumes!" Belle told her. "I brought a *ton* of clothing—so I'm helping everyone get fancy."

"Well the good news is, you can get fancy too, because you're allowed to be in the talent show! We just need to plan a group routine," JoJo explained.

"Amazing," Belle giggled. "I've been simply dying to wear this, dahling." She popped a tiara on her head and pulled a giant, lacy tutu over her cutoffs.

Bahi's eyes widened. "Um, Belle? You brought *all that* to camp?!"

"A girl's gotta be prepared," Belle told them, cutting the toes off a pair of purple polka-dot knee socks to make leg warmers for Mitzi. "Right, Mitzi? You never know when there will be a fashion emergency." The little camper beamed in response.

"Or when you won't want to wear an orange Art Stars T-shirt," Bahi teased.

"What should we do for our performance?" Miley piped in.

"What about a skit?" suggested Reagan.

"But I want to sing!" said Sydney.

"And I want to dance!" Liz called out.

"And truthfully, I want to choreograph!" chimed in Miley.

JoJo laughed. "At least we all know we're doing what we love!" she said. "What about . . . a musical?"

Belle clapped her hands. "Amazing! And since I can't really do anything onstage, I can produce and direct. Maybe song write too," she said. "Have I ever told you I possess a natural knack for song writing?" JoJo saw the other girls deflate. Belle was taking over all the roles!

"You know what, Belle? I think you'd be amazing at costume design," JoJo suggested. "You're clearly a natural."

"Oh em gee. You're right. I am. Thanks, JoJo. I'll be head costume designer!"

"Sounds perfect," JoJo said, and Bahi laughed and ruffled her friend's hair. JoJo was glad Belle was up to her old tricks . . . but in a nicer, more team-player way.

"Okay, I have an idea," JoJo told the group. "Here's what we're going to do . . ."

They all huddled together while she detailed her plan.

"Brilliant," Miley said when she was done. "Seriously, JoJo. Brilliant."

A few hours later, the girls were gathered on a dimly lit stage in the party barn behind a long black curtain. They were decked out in black tights, yellow leg warmers, black leotards (or tank tops and shorts, for some), and black-and-yellow accessories, including bright yellow bows. As the curtain began to rise, Belle's voice filled the room through an off-stage microphone.

"Do you know why the queen bee is so amazing?" she asked the audience. There were a couple of confused chuckles. "Is it because she's in charge?" she asked.

"No!" shouted the bees—a.k.a. the campers onstage—as the curtain rose to reveal their honeybee costumes.

"Is it because she's special?" Belle's voice asked.

"NO WAY!" shouted the bees.

"Then why?" Belle wondered into the microphone.

"I know," said Reagan, loud and clear into a standing mic on the stage. "It's because of her hive!"

At this, all the bees onstage raised their wings and started to sing. "We work together!" they belted out. "We adapt! And we communicate!"

"*How* do you communicate?" Belle broke in, as if she really didn't know.

"We DANCE!" the girls shouted in unison. Then they broke into dance, courtesy of Miley's spectacular choreography.

The girls nailed their moves, and Miley left a beat in the middle for freestyling. When all the kids broke into their individual talents, the audience whooped and applauded. Come to think of it, JoJo thought to herself as she danced across the stage with her bunkmates, bees were an awful lot like Siwanatorz!

When Sydney faux-stung Jamilla, everyone giggled. Soon they were singing along to the girls' "work together" refrain, which was set to the tune of a Beyoncé song, because of course.

At the very end of the routine, all the girls hopped off the stage and buzzed around the audience, who laughed and applauded. Then, when things had quieted down, Belle said into the microphone, "We'd like to thank our very own queen bee, Bethany! Bethany, come get your crown!" Bethany stood and made her way to Belle's position at the side of the stage. She bent and gave Belle a huge hug, then accepted the tiara Belle offered.

"I'm so proud of you girls," she said, sounding a little teary.

"Three cheers to the best leader of all—and my hero," said Belle. "You taught me what it means to be part of a hive."

The audience roared.

And then the next act went onstage.

All the routines were incredible, thought JoJo, as she watched the other campers perform under the guidance of their supertalented counselors. But theirs? Theirs had

112

truly been the best version of itself ... all because they'd worked together. Being the best alone wasn't nearly as fun as being the best together, JoJo realized. She hoped Belle felt the same way.

JoJo was lugging her bag to the parking lot toward Miley's mom's waiting car, when Belle jogged up to her. Miley was already in the backseat.

"JoJo, do you have a sec?"

"Of course," JoJo replied. Belle looked nervous—JoJo could tell she had something important to say.

"My parents and I just spoke with Bethany, and she told us I won't be allowed to return to any Art Stars events as a mentor," she said, her voice quiet. "The other girls don't know yet."

"I'm sorry, Belle," JoJo said. She could tell how disappointed Belle was. "I know Miley will miss seeing you at future events."

"I know I deserve it," Belle said. "How can I be a mentor to younger girls if I'm misbehaving? But it's really disappointing. It's definitely a lesson."

JoJo nodded. She didn't know what to say. It seemed like Belle hadn't ever had to learn the hard way until now. She knew the younger girls loved Belle and would miss seeing her, but she understood Bethany's choice.

"I did want to say how grateful I am to you for sticking up for me—I was so glad to be a part of the talent show with everyone else. So thank you for that."

"Of course!" JoJo exclaimed. "It turned out perfect. And hey, let's keep in touch." She pulled out her phone and handed it to Belle, so she could put her number in. Belle's face brightened.

"Thanks, JoJo!" She typed in her information and handed the phone back. "I'd love to stay in touch." Then she gave JoJo a big hug, and JoJo joined Miley in the backseat of her mom's car.

"That was sweet," Miley said, when JoJo slid in next to her. "What were you guys talking about?"

"We exchanged phone numbers," JoJo replied. She didn't want to mention what had happened with Bethany. That was Belle's news to share with Miley when she was ready. "I'm glad we're friends now."

"Yeah," Miley agreed. "Who'd have predicted that?"

JoJo smiled and shrugged. Life was full of good surprises if you kept yourself open.

CHAPTER 9

"**Y**ou girls were terrific," Miley's mom told them a few minutes later. "And that slideshow was a hoot. I took a video of the whole thing for your mom, JoJo. Did you girls have fun at camp?"

"Oh em gee, camp was so crazy," Miley said. "I had fun, but I'm excited to get back to regular life!"

"And BowBow!" said JoJo.

"And Dusty!" said Miley.

"And Jacob and Kyra and Grace!" said JoJo. She missed her other friends a lot.

"I wonder what our next adventure together will be?" Miley mused as the SUV left behind the tree-lined gravel roads leading to camp to connect with the freeway.

JoJo shrugged. "I don't know. But I'm ready!" she said. "And you've got more Art Stars events coming up, right? This weekend was just the beginning."

"Next month we're going to watch Irish step dancers perform, then afterward there's a workshop with their choreographer," Miley told her. "I can't wait. I've never studied Irish step dance."

"So cool," JoJo agreed.

Just then, JoJo's phone buzzed. She pulled

it out of her pocket to check her new text. It was a group chain.

<3 ya, Belle had written. *Missing my hive already.*

Xoxoxo, wrote Jamilla.

JoJo typed out, *Had so much fun w my girls!* and added Miley to the chain.

Bahi added a kissy-face emoji . . .

And Miley finished it off with a row of yellow hearts.

Then Belle wrote, *Siwanatorz 4 lyfe* and included a gif of Beyoncé onstage with the words, "Y'all be good, Beyhive!" written below.

"What are you two giggling about back there?" Miley's mom wanted to know.

"Oh, nothing," Miley said, just as JoJo replied, "Camp stuff."

"Okaaay," Miley's mom replied, but she was smiling. "Make any new friends?"

"Oh, yes," JoJo replied.

"The best," Miley said. "Thanks for sending us to camp, Mom."

A couple of hours later, they pulled into JoJo's driveway. JoJo's mom opened the front door and stepped out onto the lawn, beaming. BowBow scampered after her and ran circles around her feet, then yipped at the parked car. JoJo flung open the door and ran to her mom, wrapping her in a huge hug.

"Missed you!" she said.

"Missed *you*," her mom replied. "You're never allowed to leave again! I'm kidding," she said, laughing. "But I missed my bedazzling buddy."

JoJo felt BowBow's paws scrabbling at her ankle.

"Aww, BowBow," she said, bending to scoop

up the little dog. "Did you think I forgot about you? Never!" She gave BowBow a kiss on her wet nose.

Miley stepped out of the car and handed JoJo her backpack and sleeping bag, while Miley's mom chatted with Mrs. Siwa through the window.

"You're my favorite," Miley told JoJo, giving her a hug. "I'm so glad we're best pals."

"Samesies," JoJo replied. "Thanks for inviting me! That was one crazy weekend."

"Crazy-fun," Miley corrected.

"Totally. I'm down for another camping weekend anytime." JoJo gave Miley one last squeeze, then Miley hopped back in the car and buckled up.

JoJo and her mom stood in the front yard, waving as Miley and her mom pulled away.

"Phew," JoJo said, stepping into their foyer. "I need a nap! I am wiped out."

"You go rest while I get dinner together," her mom told her. "I thought we could order pizza—your favorite!"

"UGH NO," JoJo replied. "And believe me when I say I never thought I'd utter those words about pizza!"

"Pizza overload this weekend?" JoJo's mom laughed. "No worries. How about some good, old-fashioned spaghetti and meatballs?"

"Yes, please," JoJo told her. "I'll be down in a bit." Then she and BowBow made their way up to her room, where she sank into her cozy pink bed. BowBow curled up on her pillow next to her head.

"*You* didn't have the exhausting weekend, BowBow!" JoJo giggled, scratching her pup behind the ears. "But man. That's enough adventure for me for a while."

JoJo was just beginning to doze off when her phone buzzed again. Then again.

She rolled over and lifted it from her nightstand, where it was charging. It was Michelle Lee, her ice dancing friend from the dance workshop! JoJo sat up, excited. She hadn't heard from Michelle in a while.

Hey girl, read the text. *Sounds like I missed an awesome weekend! So sad* ☹

JoJo was about to type back, but the typing bubble popped back up.

What are you doing next month? Are you up for another adventure?

Another adventure? With Michelle Lee? JoJo was 100 percent in.

Always, she typed back. *What did you have in mind?*

Well, I was asked to perform at an indoor arena near the beach . . . lol. I know ice-skating at the beach is so crazy, Michelle typed . . .

JoJo settled back and typed away to her friend, a brilliant plan already taking form.

MORE BOOKS AVAILABLE BY JOJO SIWA!

MORE BOOKS AVAILABLE BY JOJO SIWA!

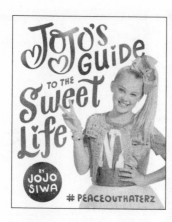